# The Wishing Stone

by Steve Smallman
Illustrated by Rebecca Elliott

QED

Armadillo lived in the swamp.

He was lonely and wished that
he could find a friend.

But whenever anyone came near him,
he would roll himself up into a ball
and keep very still until they went away.

"What shall we play today?" squeaked Mouse. "Hide and seek?"

"No, I always lose," grumbled Flamingo.

"I know... **WATER FIGHT!**" shouted Monkey, and he pushed Flamingo into the swamp and jumped in after her.

Mouse couldn't swim, so he sat down grumpily on a funny-looking stone.

"I wish I had a paddling pool so I could play, too," he said quietly.

That night, Armadillo
set to work.

Using his strong claws,
he dug a wide hole and
filled it with water.

Then, tired out, he rolled
into a ball and went to sleep.

"A paddling pool!" squeaked
Mouse excitedly the next morning.

"My wish came true.
That stone must be magic!"

"Let me try," said Flamingo, sitting on the stone. "I wish we had a secret den," she said.

"You'll have to wait until tomorrow for it to work," said Mouse.

That night, Armadillo
worked hard.

He cut down branches and
collected leaves, and by the time
the sun started to rise, he had
made a wonderful secret den.

Tired out, he rolled into
a ball and went to sleep.

"The wishing stone worked!" squawked Flamingo the next day, climbing inside the secret den.

"My turn!" cried Monkey, sitting on the stone. "I wish there was some food in here!"

"That's a stupid wish," said Flamingo.

"Not if you're hungry," said Monkey.

"But you'll have to wait until tomorrow for it to work, silly," said Mouse.

Armadillo liked
to eat bugs.

So that night, he dug a hole inside the den,
lined it with leaves and then filled it with all
the tastiest-looking bugs he could find.

Then, tired out, he rolled
into a ball and went to sleep.

"Yuck!" Monkey, Flamingo and Mouse
didn't like bugs.

"That wishing stone is useless!"
shouted Monkey, and kicked it towards the
deepest part of the swamp.

"HELP!" cried Armadillo,
as he rolled faster and faster.
"I can't swim!" SPLASH!

"The wishing stone talks," gasped Mouse. "And it can't swim!"

Monkey found a big stick and pushed it into the water.

Armadillo grabbed it and the three friends pulled with all their strength until...

PLOP!

Out came Armadillo, soggy and gasping for breath.

"Did you make my paddling pool?" asked Mouse.

"And our den?" added Flamingo. Armadillo nodded.

"What about the bugs?" asked Monkey.

"They're my favourite," sniffed Armadillo.
"I thought you would like them, too."

"Thank you. You're very kind," they replied, smiling.

Mouse, Flamingo, Monkey and Armadillo
soon became firm friends.

With Monkey's help, Armadillo learned to swim.
He even let Mouse ride on his back
in the deep end.

"Maybe wishes do come true,"
Armadillo thought happily.

# Notes for parents and teachers

- Look at the front cover of the book together. Can the children guess what the story might be about? Read the title together. Does this give them more of a clue or make it more confusing?

- What words could the children use to describe the armadillo?

- Why is he so kind to the other animals? Are they kind to him? Ask the children to talk about someone they are kind to. Who is kind to them? Why is kindness important?

- Armadillos like to eat bugs. What do the children think the other animals like to eat? Ask the children to draw pictures of their favourite foods.

- At the end of the story, Armadillo thinks that wishes do come true. Can the children remember what he wished for at the beginning of the story? If the children could make a wish, what would they wish for, and why?

- Discuss what it feels like to be lonely or 'left out' and about different ways to make friends. Talk about why it's also important to include new friends.

Copyright © QED Publishing 2010

First published in the UK in 2010 by QED Publishing
A Quarto Group Company
226 City Road
London EC1V 2TT

www.qed-publishing.co.uk

ISBN 978 1 84835 436 4

Printed in China

A catalogue record for this book is available from the British Library.

Editor: Amanda Askew
Designers: Vida and Luke Kelly